The Thirsty Crow

An imprint of Om Books International

On a bright summer morning, a crow flew around looking for water. It was a very hot day and there seemed to be no water anywhere. The ponds that he usually went to had all dried up.

He had been going around for quite some time now and was very thirsty. He thought, "I need to find water very soon or I am sure I will not be able to fly anymore." He decided to fly in a new direction. As he flew by some trees, he saw a beautiful garden.

The crow flew above the garden, eagerly looking for water. "There must be water somewhere for all these lovely flowers and trees," he said to himself. He flew lower and, as expected, he saw a pitcher standing in a part of the garden.

The crow swooped down to the pitcher swiftly, wishing that it would not be empty. He stood on its rim and looked in. He was lucky. There was water. Quickly he put his beak inside the pitcher to drink water, but found that he could not. What was the problem? Was there any water there or had he imagined it? He looked inside again carefully.

Yes, there was water, but because there was so little of it, he could not reach it with his beak. He tried again but with no luck. He hopped to the other side of the rim and tried very hard, again and again, but he could not reach the water.

The crow looked around in disappointment. There was no water to be seen anywhere else. He started to get very worried. He cawed loudly, "If I do not get any water to drink immediately, I will die of thirst! I must do something very fast."

He flew down to the ground and gave the pitcher a push. He thought that if he could overturn it, the water would flow out and he would be able to drink it easily. But the pitcher was too heavy. He tried hard with all his little strength but he could not even move it from its place.

Suddenly, he noticed some pebbles lying around the pitcher. He had an idea. He picked one pebble up in his beak. He flew back up to the rim of the pitcher and dropped the pebble inside. The water splashed up. He dropped another pebble and the water splashed up again. The crow started getting excited.

One by one he put in more pebbles, and as each pebble was dropped, the water began rising. Soon, the level of the water in the pitcher was high enough for him to reach. He bent down and drank merrily till his stomach was full. Finally! He was able to satisfy his thirst.

He was so glad that he had not given up, for if he had done so, he might not have been able to save his own life. "Yes, hard work really pays," said the crow to himself as he flew away high into the sky.